THE
THREE LITTLE PIGS
AND THE FOX
AN APPALACHIAN TALE

WILLIAM H. HOOKS

ILLUSTRATED BY

S. D. SCHINDLER

ALADDIN PAPERBACKS

For William Pierce Haar
—W.H.H.

To Chip, Martha, and Mark—
Three Little Piggies who aren't
fooled by the Fox
— S.D.S.

25 Years of Magical Reading

ALADDIN PAPERBACKS
EST. 1972

First Aladdin Paperbacks edition 1997
Text copyright © 1989 by William H. Hooks
Illustrations copyright © 1989 by S. D. Schindler

Aladdin Paperbacks
An imprint of Simon & Schuster
Children's Publishing Division
1230 Avenue of the Americas
New York, NY 10020

Also available in a Simon & Schuster Books for Young Readers edition.
The text of this book was set in 15 point Cheltenham Old Style.
The illustrations were done in watercolor.
Printed and bound in Singapore

10 9 8 7 6 5 4 3 2 1

The Library of Congress has cataloged the hardcover edition as follows:

Hooks, William H.
The three little pigs and the fox/William H. Hooks
illustrated by S. D. Schindler.—1st American ed.
p. cm.
Summary: In this Appalachian version of the classic tale, Hamlet,
the youngest pig, rescues her two greedy brothers from the clutches of the
"mean, tricky old drooly-mouth fox."
ISBN 0-02-744431-7
[1. Folklore—United States. 2. Pigs—Folklore.] I. Schindler, S. D., ill.
II. Three little pigs. III. Title.
PZ8.1.H8525Th 1989 398.2'4529734—dc19 [E] 88-29296 CIP AC

ISBN 0-689-80962-X (Aladdin pbk.)

AUTHOR'S NOTE

The art of storytelling is alive and well in Appalachia. It has flourished there since the earliest English, Scottish, and Irish settlers arrived more than three centuries ago. The classic folk and fairy tales have been preserved, but gradually in the telling they have changed until they seem to spring not from some fanciful, faraway place, but from the mountains and hollows of Appalachia itself.

Each storyteller is unique, adding local color and regional language to capture and enchant an audience. This rendition of *The Three Little Pigs* is based on several oral versions I have heard over the years in the Great Smoky Mountains. In keeping with one of the truest roles of the storyteller, I have added a few flourishes of my own.

This story happened a long time ago, way back when the animals could still talk around these parts. Back then they could say a whole lot more than *baa-baa*, *moo-moo*, *oink-oink*, and stuff like that. They could talk just like human folks.

Back then there was this humongous mama pig. She built herself a house out of rocks in a pretty green holler over Black Mountain way. As soon as she'd finished, she moved into her fine rock house with her three piglets.

The oldest piglet, Rooter, was a fair-sized shoat.
The middle piglet, Oinky, was a real mama's boy.
The baby piglet was a tiny little girl runt named Hamlet.

Now, Rooter and Oinky and Hamlet had the finest pig house in the holler. They even had a wallowing hole right in the front yard. But all Rooter and Oinky wanted to do was eat, eat, eat!

Baby Hamlet liked to eat, too—but not all the time. Hamlet liked to roll around in the delicious mud in the wallowing hole and look up at the pretty blue sky. She was a right smart piglet with more on her mind than eating.

It wasn't long 'fore Rooter and Oinky got so fat they just about filled up the whole house. What a squeeze it was to fit everybody in.

Finally it got so tight that Mama Pig spoke to Rooter. "Rooter, you're the oldest. Time's come for you to go out and seek your fortune."

"Oh, no!" Rooter squealed. "I'm still a piglet!"

"Look in that mudhole," said Mama Pig. "What do you see?"

Rooter looked in the muddy water. "I see a great big fat pig," he said.

"That big fat pig is you, Rooter. Time's come to go out and seek your fortune."

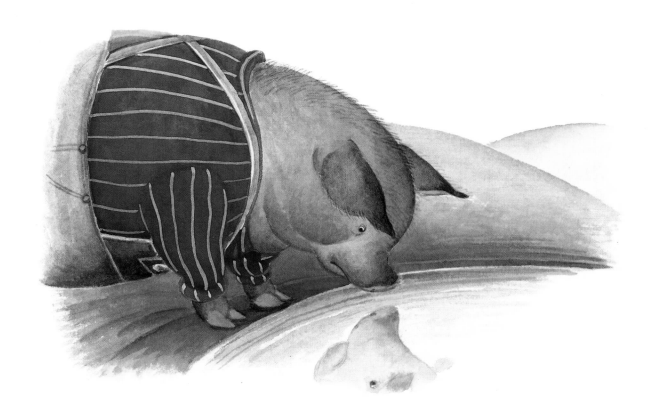

Well, Rooter hemmed and hawed and had an extra big helping of his mama's baked beans to settle his nerves. Oinky had some, too, just to keep Rooter company.

Meanwhile, Mama Pig gathered up some hoecakes and turnips, along with some dried beans and corn. She packed them in a big tow sack for Rooter to take along.

"Now, son," said Mama Pig, "you'll be fine if you remember three things."

"That's a lot to remember," said Rooter.

"Stop chewing and listen careful," said Mama Pig.

Rooter gulped. "I'm listening."

"One: You got to watch out for that mean, tricky old drooly-mouth fox.

"Two: Build yourself a safe, strong house out of rocks.

"Three: Come home to see your mama every single Sunday."

Mama and Oinky and baby Hamlet kissed Rooter on his fat, round jowls. And for good luck they kissed him again on his pink, trembly snout.

Then Rooter trotted on down the road, dragging his tow sack behind him. He walked and he walked. And what did all that walking do? It made him mighty hungry.

He didn't think about any mean, tricky old drooly-mouth fox.

He didn't think about any safe, strong rock house.

He didn't think about visiting his mama come Sunday.

All he could think about was the food his mama had put into the tow sack. So he set himself down on a rock and opened up the sack.

"Hoecakes!" He squealed and started gobbling them up.

Rooter felt a tap on the shoulder. He didn't look around, and he didn't miss a chew, just said between bites, "Don't bother me. I'm busy eating."

But the tapping went on. Rooter swallowed a big chunk of hoecake and looked around. There was mean, tricky old drooly-mouth fox grinning at him.

"Have some hoecake," said Rooter, real scared.

"Don't like hoecake," said the fox.

"Well, how about some turnips or corn?" said Rooter.

"Don't like none of them," said the fox.

"Well, what can I offer you?" asked Rooter.

"I love barbecued pig!" cried the fox. And he grabbed the tow sack and stuffed Rooter into it.

"Please don't eat me up," Rooter pleaded.

"I won't eat you right now," said mean, tricky old droolymouth fox. "I'm going to save you up for a cold winter's day. Nothing like hot barbecue on a cold winter's day."

So he took poor Rooter off to his den and locked him up.

Sunday rolled around. All day Mama Pig and baby Hamlet looked for Rooter to come visiting, while Oinky spent the Sabbath eating a double share of rutabagas and corn dumplings. But the night came on without Rooter ever showing up.

A month of Sundays passed, and they didn't see snout or tail of Rooter. Meanwhile, Oinky was growing so big the house was getting crowded again. They were having a hard time fitting in.

Finally Mama Pig said, "Oinky, it's time you set out to seek your fortune."

"No, Mama!" Oinky squealed. "I'm too little to leave my mama."

"Look in that mud hole and tell me what you see," said Mama Pig.

Oinky looked in the muddy water and saw how huge he had grown. He knew his mama was right. Oinky didn't say a word, but two big tears rolled down his plump jowls.

Mama Pig said, "No need for tears, Oinky. All you have to do is remember three things.

"One: Watch out for that mean, tricky old drooly-mouth fox.

"Two: Build yourself a safe, strong house out of rocks.

"Three: Come home to see your mama every single Sunday."

Mama packed Oinky a tow sack full of his favorite food, rutabagas and corn dumplings.

Then baby Hamlet and Mama Pig kissed Oinky on his fat, round jowls. And for good luck they kissed him again on his pink, trembly snout.

Oinky went slowly on down the road till he was out of sight. He walked and he walked. And he kept thinking how much he was going to miss his mama. He felt so sad, he sat down on a rock to have a little nourishment and cheer himself. He didn't think once about the mean fox or building a safe house, although he did long for Sunday to visit his mama.

Oinky was just easing a tooth into a crusty, golden corn dumpling when he felt a tap on the shoulder. He whirled around so fast he dropped the dumpling. There was mean, tricky old drooly-mouth fox grinning at him.

"Would you like some of my dumplings?" stammered Oinky, scared to death.

"Never eat 'em," said the fox.

"How about some rutabagas?" asked Oinky.

"Can't stand the smell of 'em," said the fox.

"Well, what do you like?" asked Oinky.

"Pork with lima beans!" said the fox. And he snatched up the tow sack and stuffed poor Oinky inside.

"Please don't eat me," begged Oinky. "Please! Please! Please!"

"Oh, shut up," said mean, tricky old drooly-mouth fox. "I'm not going to eat you right now. I'm going to save you for a rainy day. There's nothing better than pork and beans on a rainy day."

So the fox took Oinky to his den and locked him up.

Sunday rolled around. Mama and baby Hamlet got up early and cooked a big mess of collard greens and wild onions. They wanted to have something special in case Rooter and Oinky remembered to come see their mama. But the night came on without either Rooter or Oinky ever showing up.

A month of Sundays passed, and they didn't see snout or
tail of Rooter or Oinky. The leaves turned all red and gold,
and the nights got real nippy.

Baby Hamlet—who didn't look so much like a little runt
anymore—was getting restless. One day she spoke to her
mama. "Mama, it's high time I set out to seek my fortune."

"No, no!" Mama Pig cried. "You're too young to leave
your mama! Besides, none of my children ever come back to
visit me on Sundays."

"Now, stop your worrying, Mama," said Hamlet. "I can take care of myself. All I've got to do is remember three things.

"One: Watch out for that mean, tricky old drooly-mouth fox.

"Two: Build myself a safe, strong house out of rocks.

"Three: Come home and visit my dear, sweet mama every Sunday."

So Mama Pig packed a tow sack with sweet potato pone, Hamlet's favorite food. She kissed baby Hamlet on her fat, round jowls, and for luck kissed her again on her pink, trembly snout.

Hamlet skipped on down the road. She walked and she walked. She looked all around to make sure no mean fox was sneaking up on her. She got tired and set herself down on a rock to rest.

"I think I'll just have a nibble on this sweet potato pone," she said.

Suddenly she felt a tap on the shoulder. It was mean, tricky old drooly-mouth fox grinning at her.

"What a surprise!" exclaimed Hamlet. She was thinking fast and stalling for time.

"I've got a real big surprise for you," said the fox.

"I mentioned *surprise* first," said Hamlet. "This tow sack is full of surprises."

The fox reached inside the sack and pulled out some sweet potato pone. "Umm," he mumbled, chewing away. "Only one thing I like better than sweet potato pone."

"What's that?" asked Hamlet.

"Pork chops to go with it!" cried the fox, grabbing for baby Hamlet.

But Hamlet was too sharp for him. She slapped the tow sack over the fox and tied it tight with a hard knot. Then she left that old fox rolling and squirming around on the ground inside the sack.

Hamlet skipped on down the road till she found a place with a fine bunch of rocks. She made herself a safe little rock house with a nice fireplace to keep warm by.

No sooner had Hamlet settled in than that mean, tricky old drooly-mouth fox came knocking at her door. "Please let me in, little pig," he begged. "I'm near freezing to death."

"Not on the fuzz of your bushy tail will I let you in," said Hamlet.

"Please, have mercy on a poor old fox. My nose is about frozen off. Just open the door a crack to let me warm my nose," he pleaded.

Hamlet cracked the door a mite. The fox shoved his nose in the crack.

Slam! Hamlet banged the door shut.

The fox thought his nose would really drop off, it hurt so. But he was thinking what nice pork chops Hamlet would make.

"My nose is warmer now," he called, "but my ears are freezing. Please open the door a little wider so I can warm my ears."

Hamlet opened the door a little more. The fox tried to push all the way in.

Slam! Hamlet banged the door shut, pretty near knocking the breath out of mean, tricky old drooly-mouth fox.

But the fox still had his mind set on pork chops.

"Oh, that was much better, little pig." He gasped. "Now, if you would open the door a little bit more and let me get my hind feet warmed, I'll be on my way."

Hamlet opened the door wide. The fox sprang inside. But that smart little pig was too fast for him. *Slam!* She shut the door on his tail and stopped him in his tracks.

"Oh, oh, my tail!" cried mean, tricky old drooly-mouth fox.

"Shut up!" said Hamlet. "You're making so much racket I can't hear what's going on outside."

The fox lowered his voice to a moan. "Please, my tail. My tail."

"Just what I thought I heard," said Hamlet. "Dogs barking."

"Dogs? What kind of dogs?" asked the fox.

"Hunting dogs. I'm sure they're fox-hunting dogs, from the way they're barking."

"Please hide me," cried the fox. "Don't let the hounds catch me!"

Hamlet was thinking fast and sharp.

"I'll hide you if you tell me what you've done with Rooter and Oinky."

"They're locked up in my den. Please, hurry. Those dogs will be here any minute."

"First tell me where I can find your den."

Mean, tricky old drooly-mouth fox hated to give that away. But his tail was killing him, and the dogs were hot on his trail.

"It's under the big, rusty-colored rock over in Rattlesnake Holler." He groaned.

"Here, jump into this churn," said Hamlet. She pushed the door off mean, tricky old drooly-mouth fox's tail and lifted the lid from the big wooden churn.

The fox squeezed inside. Hamlet slammed the lid down on the churn and latched it tight.

"Are the dogs getting closer?" the fox mumbled from inside the churn.

"What dogs?" asked baby Hamlet. "I don't hear any dogs."

The old fox knew he'd been tricked. He gnashed his teeth and rattled and raved and shook the churn. But he couldn't get out.

Baby Hamlet rolled the churn down to the creek and right into the water. Downstream it floated like an ark. And that was the last mean, tricky old drooly-mouth fox was seen around the hollers of Black Mountain.

Baby Hamlet hurried on down to Rattlesnake Holler and searched all around till she found the fox den with her brothers, Rooter and Oinky.

It just happened to be on a Sunday when she found them and set them free. So they all trotted right over to Mama Pig's house. And there was snorting and eating, and kissing and eating, and wallowing in the mud hole and more eating, the likes of which you've never seen.